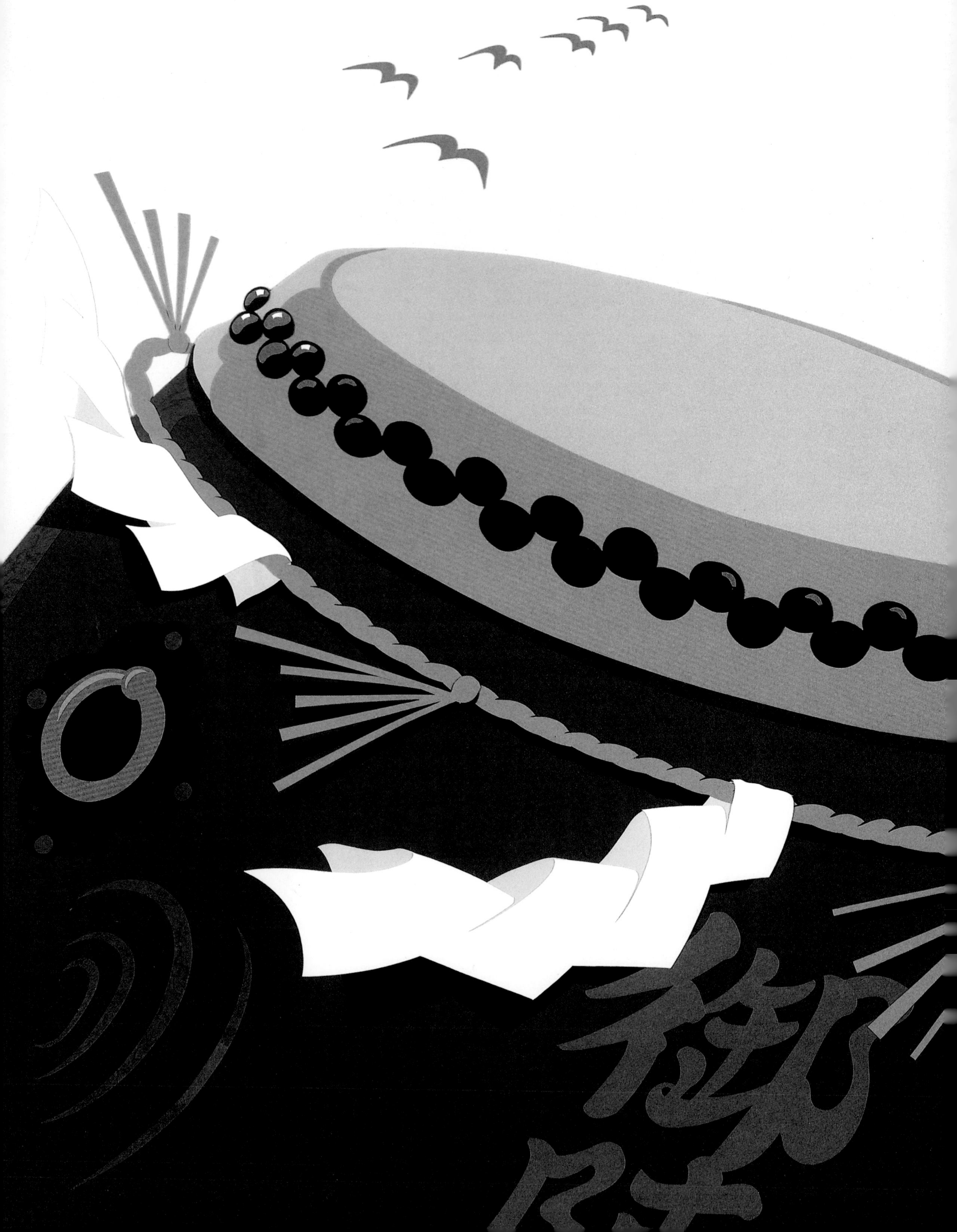

The Drums of Noto Hanto

story *by* **J. Alison James**

illustrations by **Tsukushi**

A Dorling Kindersley Book

Dorling Kindersley
LONDON, NEW YORK, SYDNEY, DELHI, PARIS, MUNICH and JOHANNESBURG

First published in Great Britain in 2000 by Dorling Kindersley Limited,
9 Henrietta Street, London WC2E 8PS

2 4 6 8 10 9 7 5 3 1

First published in 1999 by DK Ink, an imprint of Dorling Kindersley Publishing, Inc.,
95 Madison Avenue, New York, NY 10016, USA

A CIP catalogue record for this book is available from the British Library.

ISBN 0-7513-7227-7

Printed and bound in China

For our complete
catalogue visit
www.dk.com

Noto Hanto points upwards like a thumb into the Sea of Japan. Even its rocks are wild, carved by the waves and great winds of typhoons. Today few people live there, where their ancestors cut rice fields from the steep sides of the hills. Their lives are much the same as they have been for centuries: planting rice, catching fish, harvesting rice – and, at each change of season, playing the drums.

And at harvest time, they dance for the ghosts
of their ancestors and play on the drums:
Tiki tiki tiki tiki ton ton ton
Podo pada Podo pada
Koto Koto Ko
DON kada DON kada DON DON DON!

Many, many years ago, a powerful warlord named Kenshin threatened the people of Nabune village. It was known far beyond Noto Hanto as the wealthiest village on the coast. The people there had the best fishing, the best mountain vegetables, good hunting, and the most delicious rice.

Kenshin wanted their rice crop in taxes. He wanted to taste their fish. He wanted their fathers and young men for soldiers. He sent his samurai warriors on ships to conquer them and claim their riches.

The rice had been harvested when a messenger rode over the hills and into the village. He had news – the samurai were coming. They were coming by sea and would attack from the bay!

Frantically the villagers collected what weapons they had. But these were only a farmer's scythe, a hunter's spear, a fisherman's harpoon. What use could they be against the swords of the warriors?

"We can never outfight the samurai," one man said.
"All is lost," cried a woman.
But an old man said, "Go get the drums. If we cannot fight them, perhaps we can trick them."
The children scattered one way, their parents another.

They brought all the drums
down to the beach:
Small high-voiced drums and
sharp metal bells –
Ton ton ton ton Tiki tiki tik!

Middle-sized drums that
shook the leaves on the trees –
Podo pada Podo pada
Koto koto Ko!

Large drums that boomed like thunder –

DON kada DON kada DON DON DON!

And they brought the great Taiko, a drum so huge that eight men could play it at the same time. It was covered by a stretched skin fastened with hundreds of nails. When that drum was pounded, it sounded like a mountain exploding:

DON DON DON DON!

The villagers hid the drums and piled up
wood for fires.

Suddenly someone shrieked with fear:
"Giyaa!"

Emerging from the woods were wild monsters
with wide blank eyes and long green hair and
skin covered with welts. The monsters ran
towards the beach . . .

It was the children running, wearing masks.
"Ah," the old man cried. They had fooled everyone.
The drums, the fires, and now these monster faces –
would not the samurai melt with fear?

The villagers scattered again. Some went into the
woods and sliced off great pieces of tree bark. Some ran
down along the shore and pulled up tangles of stringy
seaweed. Some gathered handfuls of white hair from the
tail of the messenger's horse.

Swiftly they made terrifying masks.

As the sun sank into the sea, four huge ships rounded
the cliff into the bay. Their sides were lined with oars.
On their decks a thousand swords flashed red.
The villagers stood awestruck on the beach.

Then someone took courage and,
running, lit the fires.

The sharp metal bell
called the drummers to play:
Tiki tiki tiki tiki tik!
The children, and then everyone,
covered their faces with masks.

DON da DON da DON
domba domba domba DON!

Already the fires were spitting flames.
Louder and louder the villagers
pounded the drums:

The ships slowed on the darkening water. A rain of arrows came. But the drums called an answer.

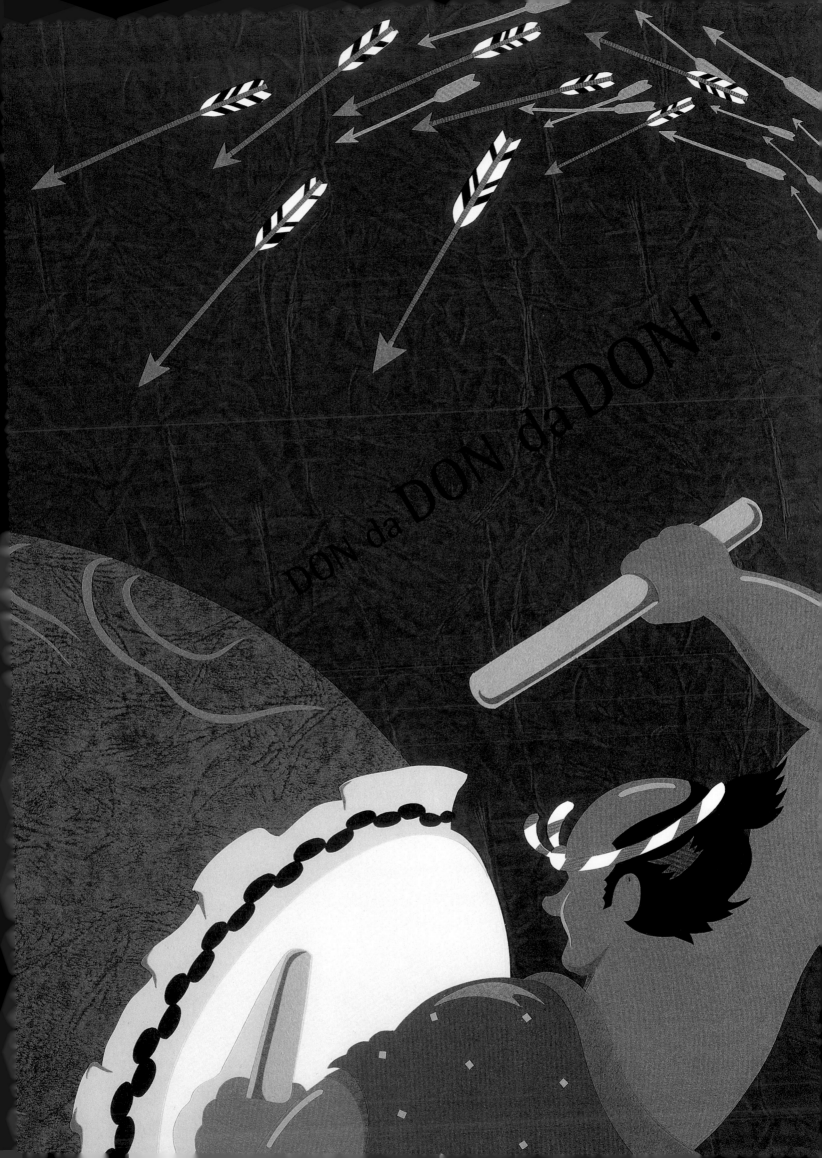

The light of the fires licked the waves.

DON tonga DON tonga DON! DON! DON!
TIKI TIKI TIKI TIKI TIKI TIKI TIK!

The gruesome monsters danced.

All night the villagers drummed – the sound pounded like blood in the ears of the samurai.

All night the ships sat on the sea. But they came no closer, even as the sun rose. For on the beach, hideous monsters loomed from the mists of the sea. As the drums boomed, the monsters came shouting down into the water, shaking with fury. And behind them, the great Taiko sounded so loud and low that the ocean itself seemed to tremble.

DON DON DON DON!

"Back!" came the call from one of the ships, and the oars sliced the water like swords. The villagers waited until the mist cleared and the birds could be heard over the echo of the drums. They waited and watched as the samurai ships faded in the distance, never to return.

Since the year 1576, the people of Noto Hanto have celebrated their ancestors' victory over the samurai. In a festival each summer they play the drums and wear masks of bark and seaweed. The masks are frightening, but it is the beat of the drums that stalls the beat of the heart:

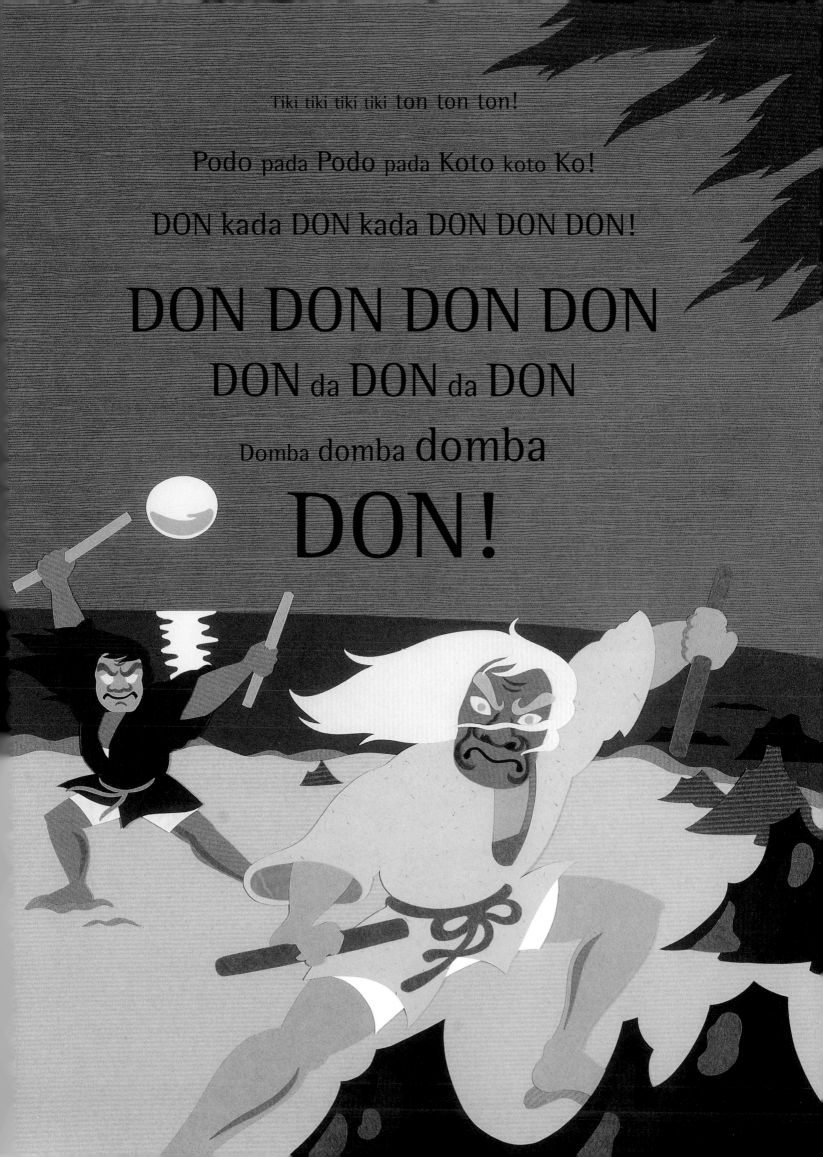